# Contents

# Chapter 1
# After the Battle

It was my brave dog, Cho, who rescued me in the battle. He came to battle with me and stayed by my side. When the enemy warrior attacked, brave Cho jumped up suddenly. He growled and showed his big teeth. He looked wild and fierce. The enemy warrior had his sword at my neck but he looked away as Cho jumped up at him, and at that moment I was able to slide my own sword, my silvery katana, between his fish scale armour plates.

The warrior fell to the ground. Blood pumped from his side and turned the earth to red mud. My horse went nearly mad with fear. The howls of the dying, the smoke and the flames, and the terrible smells of battle set him in a panic.

I held on to his reins and tried to calm him down. An arrow flew out of the rolling smoke and struck Cho. The dog fell to the ground, his leg twitching. I bent down beside him and picked up the arrow. It was sharp and the tip was made of bamboo, not steel. I rubbed the very tip of the arrow with my finger, and quickly tasted it. There was no poison – Cho had been lucky.

I looked again at his leg. The wound was just a graze and not deep. I lifted my poor brave dog up and laid him across my saddle. I left my spear and banner planted in the red earth. I got back up onto my horse. His white mane flew back as we rode off. He flicked his head from side to side as we sped away from the field of battle.

There was nothing more I could have done. But even as I fled I knew I should have stayed. I was, after all, a Samurai, a warrior. It was not right for me to flee the battle. Would the gods punish me?

# Chapter 2
# The Journey and the Dead

We rode away from the battle. The land all
around us was scorched and burnt. After a long
time, we came to a different place where there
were pine trees and tall hills. At last, the smell
of fear and blood and smoke was gone. I slowed
the horse. We trotted on.

My horse grew tired. As soon as the land
around us was flat and open, I pulled him to a
stop. I got down from the saddle and stood on
the bare earth. My hound Cho limped down too.

He put his head against my leg. I pulled at his ears and stroked his faithful head. We had both been hurt in battle. We both needed to rest. The wind was strong and the grass around us was dried out and thin. There were no farms left that I could see.

Tall wooden posts, each as tall as a flag pole, had been stuck into the earth in that place. They stretched in two lines as far as the flat horizon. Each pole flew a white banner and each had a rough wooden cart-wheel fixed to the top of it. The skeletons of fallen warriors were roped and tied across the wheels. I knew that they had been left there as a warning, a warning to any man thinking of taking up arms and fighting against the Warlord. This is how they would end up, stretched across a wheel while the crows pecked at them. The crows would peck at any part of the dead and torn flesh they could see through the gaps in their armour. The banners flapped sadly in the wind. I gave a shudder, and then I clapped my hands.

A cloud of black crows rose up, screaming and cawing into the cold air. My dog yelped softly and hung his head low.

"Come on," I said to him. "We'll find food and rest soon."

The sky was grey with low dark clouds. I let Cho drink his fill from a puddle of water. The water was the colour of the sky.

I was hungry. What I wanted was a warm fire to welcome me, and someone to cook me a meal. But I knew I'd be lucky to find even a burnt out and broken down shack to shelter in. The enemy was everywhere. Would one of their soldiers find me first and kill me?

I had my armour on still. It was all hacked about and stained with the blood of the dead, but it would still protect me. I had my hunting bow too, and plenty of steel-tipped arrows. I had my huntsman's clothes made of deer skin in my saddle pack. In those I could move quickly and without a sound. I could lie low. I could hunt. I would survive somehow.

After Cho and the horse had drunk, I washed some of the blood from my armour in the puddle of water. I ripped a strip of cloth from my under-shirt and washed and bandaged poor Cho's hurt leg. The wind was wild now across the ruined plain. It was getting dark, and I needed to find shelter. The ghosts of the dead were all round me. They seemed to sigh at me from their poles. I got back up onto my horse and took hold of the reins. We needed to move on. Cho walked slowly next to me with his tail between his legs.

This was a sad and lonely place. We made our way slowly between the poles and the rotting dead corpses. At last we left the road. We passed through the ashy ruins of a town.

There were burned houses, broken fences, and the smell of death. Close by, I heard some dogs howling. It was a whole pack of dogs, too, by the sound of it. The dogs were wild. They were the last of the town – pets and farm dogs that had been left behind. All the people were dead or had run away and the dogs were all that was left. They were out yowling and barking, baying for blood.

Further off, across a dark field, I could see the ruins of what had once been a grand house, a noble palace. We would stay there and rest. I set off across the fields towards the ruin. We crossed one field safely and came to another road. Almost at once I heard the dogs howl again and saw that they were blocking our way.

# Chapter 3
# Wild Dogs

I saw the dogs then in a pack across the roadway. Their eyes shone. Their jaws dripped. Would they kill tonight and eat at last? Was I going to be their meal? I rode forward to meet them. I dropped down from my horse and sent him away across the fields towards the ruin with a slap on his flank.

I stood still on the road. I counted seven dogs in all. There was nothing between me and them. I could smell the sickness and danger on them. I was wounded and alone but I had to face the wild dogs. My dog Cho was in no state to do battle. I took him and tied him to a stout fence post. He lay on his paws and whimpered softly. I took my sword from my belt. The dogs all ran at me at once, barking and snarling. I swung my noble blade. I quickly cut heads from bodies. There was a fountain of blood. The surviving dogs fell silent. They backed away from me. I heard Cho howling behind me. I held the sword up high above my head. The dogs stepped back further. Their shoulders hunched down. Their heads were low to the ground.

They seemed dazed at the speed of my katana, my strong sword. The dogs whimpered and I saw their rotten teeth. I jumped among them and swung the sword again and again. I sliced through their necks, I hacked at their sick and skinny bodies. I killed them one after the other. I killed them quickly. They were better off dead. I stood on the dark road with the bodies of seven dead hounds. Were they the

hounds of hell that had tracked me all the way from the battle?

# Chapter 4
# The Ruins at Night

The ruined palace still had some tiles left on the roof. It would be dry at least. My horse walked slowly over the field to me when I called him. Cho stayed by my side. He was shivering.

I went into the palace slowly. The rusty door creaked and squealed. It was empty. Soldiers had stolen everything they wanted. I found a bag of rice and some fish stock in a jar in the palace kitchen. I made a fire with some dry twigs and ate.

There was a dirty mattress in a corner. I found a bit of old torn curtain and I covered it. Cho settled at my feet. I lay my head on my saddle-bags. I was soon asleep.

I dreamt terrible dreams of battle but then I woke up suddenly. I thought I heard Cho howling. Was it more wild dogs? I got to my feet. But it was the wind that had howled, not poor Cho. He sat with his head between his paws, moaning. The wind tore through the ruined palace. The broken shutters rattled like the bones of a dead army. The thunder crashed overhead like the banging of a huge drum.

The thunder and the howling wind drove me mad. I could not sleep. Poor Cho kept as close to me as he could get.

In the morning I dressed in my hunter's clothes and shot a fat bird from the roof. I found some root vegetables in the palace kitchen garden. And I was able to catch a fish in the stream. I fed Cho, washed his sore leg and made him a bandage from some clean linen that I'd found. I rested and slept that second day.

With darkness once again came the storms and the thunder. The wind howled and screeched like a million dead souls on their way to the cave of Hell, and now there was lightning too. Great sparks and flashes crashed around the ruins. Raiden, the God of thunder, must be playing with me and tormenting me because I'd left the battle early. He'd found me hiding in the ruin licking my wounds. He was punishing me for being a coward, a defeated warrior.

# Chapter 5
# A Meeting

On the third day, I put on my armour again and rode out across the empty fields. Cho came with me and he hardly limped now. He ran ahead. He growled and snapped at anything that moved. He was getting better. I found some more vegetables. I used my bow again and shot six birds. An old man was out hunting too. He shied away from me. I was a warrior in full armour and that must have scared him.

"Don't be frightened," I said.

He came out of his hiding place. He bowed to me.

"I am not going to hurt you," I said. "What happened here? Where is everyone?"

"All gone away," the old man said. "First the army came, and then the Demon."

"Demon?" I said.

"From the sky," the old man told me. "The Demon drove all of the rest away, drove them mad."

I gave the old man one of the birds I'd shot and took the rest home. I made a good stew in a bronze pot from the kitchen.

As evening fell I made my mind up to defeat the Demon, if only for my warrior pride. At dusk, I put on my hunter's clothes. I stuck a feather in my cap and went out with Cho at my side. I looked like a farmer out hunting. I had my bow across my back and my best steel-tipped arrows in my quiver. I found a bush, and I hid behind it and waited.

# Chapter 6
# The Phantom

Before long, a great black cloud came rolling and tumbling down from the evening sky. It stopped and lay over the roof of the ruined palace. At once it was as dark as night. The cloud clung to the roof. It curled itself around the ruined chimneys and towers. The wind set up its howling and screaming. Then the thunder began. The pounding drums, the cracks that shook the ground. Then there came the sudden bright flashes and the crackles of lightning. I pulled my hat low and peeped out of the bush. I saw something red move inside the black cloud. It was a grinning red face. My heart froze – it was a thunder Demon.

I watched it as it jumped and stamped with its red claws all over the roof tiles. I watched as it kicked slates off the roof and into the wind and as it pushed loose bricks from the chimney stacks. It was out to destroy the ruin and me. Cho stayed low to the ground. Cho was a fierce and brave hunting hound, but even he was terrified by the sight of the terrible red Demon, the thunder phantom. Its eyes burned red out of the black cloud. Its claws were red too. I could not see its whole body. I watched as it scurried back and forth along the palace roof.

I stepped out from the bushes. I had my bow in my hand ready. I fixed an arrow to the string and then lifted the bow. The Demon saw me. It turned its red mask and fixed its red eyes on me. Its mouth broke into a nasty grin and it poked its head out of the rolling clouds. It roared with laughter, and the laughter was

worse than the thunder. The ground shook under my feet and Cho put his head down between his paws.

"Huntsman!" the Demon shouted. "You will not hunt me!" And he laughed again.

"I am no huntsman," I called back. I aimed my arrow. The Demon stepped forward and stood proud. There was a huge crash of thunder and a crack of lightning as the Demon laughed again. I fired my steel-tipped arrow.

The arrow flew straight and true. It went right to the heart of the Demon. The clouds shook and flew apart suddenly. They span and melted away and the darkness lifted from over the roof. There was great and sudden silence in the air, which came as a shock to my ears. A night-time stillness lay over the land. Bit by bit I began to hear crickets chirp, and then an owl hooted. I called Cho to me and we went back to the palace. We slept all night. I dreamed of nothing but a blue sky.

24

# Chapter 7
# A New Journey

When I woke the next morning the sky was exactly as it had been in my dream. I took Cho outside. It was a fine morning. The old man from the day before was out with his fishing rod.

"The thunder Demon has gone," he said, and he smiled and bowed to me.

"I killed it," I said.

He bowed to me again and then said, "Now there will be a worse demon somewhere else."

I packed my bags and set off with Cho at my side. I rode on for most of the morning. I stayed dressed in my hunter's skins. My armour was packed away across the saddle. My bow was slung across my back at the ready. We came to a small town at dusk. I could hear mournful cries and weeping from behind the closed doors of the houses. I rode down the empty main street. From every house I heard the sound of a woman crying. I could smell cooking. Smoke rose from one of the houses. I hitched my horse and tied Cho to a post. I knocked on the door.

A woman opened it. I could not see her face clearly as I peered in from the dark road, but there was the smell of cooked food, just as I had hoped.

"You are a hungry traveller," she said at once and stepped aside to let me in.

"Thank you," I said. I ducked my head and went in.

A fire burned in the fireplace. Logs crackled and sparked. A pot was hung over the flames.

"Sit down, brave warrior, you must be cold," she said. "Here, by the fire, a good fire."

"How did you know that I was a warrior?" I said.

"You look strong, and you stand tall like a warrior," she said.

She went to the pot and spooned out some soup into a wooden bowl. She was not old or young, and she wore her long hair pulled back into a ribbon. She smiled, but there was sadness in her eyes.

"Here, take this while it is hot," she said.

The soup tasted good. I drank it. I was tired from my journey. The hot soup and the warm fire made me sleepy. My eyelids felt heavy. The woman moved to take my bowl.

I was almost asleep but I made myself get up from beside the fire and handed the bowl to her with a bow. I stood tall in the room. She stood looking back at me. Her eyes shone wet in the light from the fire.

I knew that sad and empty look.

"Something terrible has happened to you," I said softly.

"To all of us here," she said.

"The war," I said and shook my head.

"No, not only the war," she said.

"Where are all the men?" I said.

"They were taken away to fight by the Warlord's army. We expect that some may return safe and well. We women did well until the winter. Since then we have been haunted by a terrible Demon. We must make a sacrifice every week. Each one of the women here has taken her daughter in a closed and covered cage and left her for the Demon." She stopped and began to cry.

"Is that why I heard the women crying and wailing when I rode into the town?" I asked.

"Yes, all have lost their daughters," the woman answered.

"Did you lose a daughter too, is that why you're weeping?" I went on.

"I'm weeping because I still have a daughter," she said.

At that moment, the door on the other side of the room slid open and a beautiful girl of

about eighteen summers stepped into the room. She bowed to me and then lifted her face. She was pale and delicate. Her hair was worn like her mother's. I was struck at once in the heart with a steel-tipped arrow of love. I could not bear to see her sacrificed. I would have to act against the Demon.

I bowed to the girl.

"This is my daughter, Misaki," the woman said and began to cry with great deep sobs.

"Misaki, the blossom, will not be a sacrifice," I said. "Where is this Demon?"

Misaki's mother pointed to a hill outside the town. She stopped crying. "I will show you," she said.

# Chapter 8
# The Cave of the Demon

Misaki's mother took me to the edge of the town. We left Cho with Misaki. The women of the town stood at the doors of their houses and watched us pass. Misaki's mother showed me a steep and rocky path. She pointed to a craggy hill which loomed over everything. There was a spring of dark looking water, which fell into a glassy black pool. Beyond the pool there was an even darker cave. The women had to leave their daughters in a cage by the pool at sunset. Misaki was due to be left there the next day.

She wept again. I sent her back and went on to the hill.

I sat down and waited at the edge of the black pool. There were no birds. No fish or frogs splashed in the still dark water. Once night fell there was total silence. There were no insects at all. Then some weird sounds came from the cave. They began with harsh short hissings and then there were odd high cries. They were ghostly sounds that set my skin crawling. This was the place of the Demon all right.

I sat as still as I could. I peered into the darkness of the cave. I stared into the cave for hours as the night stretched on but the entrance stayed as still and dark as the waters of the pool. And then I saw something. It was so big that I couldn't make it out. It looked into the night for just a moment. I tried not to move at all. I was sure it would hear my heart hammer in my chest. Now I knew what had made the noises. I also knew just what I had to do.

# Chapter 9
# I Make a Plan

The next morning I called all of the women of the town together. "I have seen the terrible thing in the cave. Only for a moment, but it was long enough for me to think that I can defeat it," I said. "I only wish I had got here earlier so that I might have saved all of your daughters' lives. I would at least like to try and save the one who is left," I added, and I bowed towards Misaki, who sat still beside me with Cho's head in her lap. The dog had grown fond of her and she was stroking his ears. Many of the women wept to hear this news. I asked them to bring me the cage.

It was made of wood and had curtains which hung inside the bars. I made sure that the curtains would hide the person inside the cage. I took Cho for a walk. I had my bow slung across my back. I shot some birds and Cho fetched them at his old speed. I talked to him as he trotted along beside me. He was better now, his leg was healed and he ran around as keen and bright eyed as ever. I told him that I needed him to be just as brave as he could be. I told him that I was about to test him in a terrible way. I said that I knew I could trust him. He would be as brave and strong as always.

# Chapter 10
# A Feast

I told no one of my plans. Misaki's mother made a feast for everyone with the birds I had hunted. Everyone made a fuss of Cho. He was petted and fussed by Misaki and given some of the best meat.

It was a grim feast. There was no laughter around the table as the sun sank lower in the sky. The women sat together without talking. They all looked so sad in their black clothes.

The time was near for Misaki to enter the cage. It sat outside the house. None of the women could bear to look at it. It made them think of their lost daughters. I took off my hunting clothes and put on my armour. I had cleaned and polished it so that there were no bloodstains any more. My horse was nervous. He shook his fine white head, he snorted, and his eyes were wide. He sensed danger.

Misaki wore a white robe. She looked especially beautiful, and especially pale. She looked like the bride of death. The cage was lifted on to a cart and my horse began to pull it. I walked the cage through the streets with Misaki inside. No one watched us leave except for Misaki's mother. She kissed her daughter and held her tight. Then she stood and watched as we left. She said nothing.

Cho ran beside the cart.

"You will need to be brave, Cho," I called to him.

Near the dark pool we stopped. I lifted the empty cage down to the ground. I opened the door of the cage. Misaki looked at me. "No," I said. I called Cho over away from a burrow he was sniffing at.

"Good dog," I said. "Good boy. Now we shall have some sport, but you must be a good dog and stay quiet." Misaki came out of the cage and I put Cho in to take her place.

"Oh, no," Misaki said.

"It's all right," I said. "Cho is a good brave dog, and a warrior. He has saved me in battle before now." She came over to the cage and she hugged Cho and kissed him on the head.

"Now, Misaki," I said, "you must go and hide in the trees."

Once Cho was still, I pulled the curtains down and tied them shut. I dragged the cage over to the dark pool and left it on a patch of scrubby grass.

"Be good, Cho," I whispered. "Be brave."

Then I went and hid myself and waited.

# Chapter 11
# The Demons

I sat in the bushes near Misaki. I had my freshly sharpened sword, my faithful katana, across my knees. It was ready, and it shone with a dull gleam in the last light of the day. It would soon be dark. Cho, the brave dog, did well. He stayed hunched and silent in the covered cage.

I thought of all of the poor girls who must have wept and wailed for their mothers as they waited in the cage for the Demon.

I knew that the terrible Demon would expect to hear those sobs. I asked Misaki if she could make weeping noises. She did so very easily.

She wailed and cried and called out for her mother. Something moved in the mouth of the cave.

I could see little there – only the darkness, even darker at the cave's mouth. And a howling began, a high mewling sound, and horrible hissing noises that set my nerves on edge. I thought I could hear one strong noise and other lesser ones calling back to it, as if there were more than one demon in the cave.

At last, something came out of the dark and sniffed the air. It was a cat, a giant hulking brute of a cat, with stripes all across its body. It was the colour of smoke and after it came two others. They were smaller and hissed and snarled and showed their teeth. The biggest demon loped over to the cage. It crept close

and put out one paw. I could see its claw.
It unhooked the door of the cage. The door
dropped down with a clatter. The two smaller
cat demons followed the big one over to the
cage. I saw their wet red tongues lick their lips.

They made no sound as the giant cat
Demon put its paw into the cage. There was a
moment of stillness.

Then Cho leapt out of the cage barking,
with his teeth shining. The cat Demon rose into
the air as if its tail had been burnt. My brave
dog tore at the huge cat Demon. He sank his
teeth in its neck. The Demon screamed. I saw
its cat form melt and its furred flesh twist and
turn in the air. The smoky colour of its fur
became smoke itself as Cho attacked it barking
and snarling and biting.

I stood at once, with an arrow ready on the
string of my bow. I fired the arrow at one of the
smaller cat demons. The arrow struck it in the
heart. It screeched and twisted up in the air. I

fired another arrow at it and then another. It fell to the ground, dead.

The second smaller cat Demon sprang at me. I felt its heavy body and its sharp claws dig into me as it knocked me back. The breath was pushed out of my body in a rush. My fine sword, my katana, dropped out of my hand. This demon was the smallest but it was still huge, far bigger than any tiger. I looked in its yellow eyes. It hissed in my face. Its eyes were narrow and I could see its sharp teeth. My dog Cho turned away from what was left of the larger cat Demon and howled like a wolf. He'd won that fight.

The cat Demon opened its mouth. It twisted its ugly head on one side and went to rip my neck. I could smell its foul breath. I looked for my sword. My hands felt around in the dust and stones. The Demon looked up suddenly as if it was surprised, and I heard the silvery swish of the katana. The Demon's head was cut off in one fast blow. The look of surprise stayed on its face as its head fell to the ground. Demon blood flooded over me in a hot, dark rush.

Misaki had killed it. She had come out from the trees when the Demon jumped at me. Now she stood above me with the katana, my sword, tight in her hands. The bodies of the demons lay dead around us. Her white gown was soaked with the Demon's blood which then burned off from us both like smoke. My dog came and rested his head against my hand and I stroked his ears. We stood for a moment with the terrible bodies around us. We stood still. I took Misaki's hand and she looked up at me.

"Thank you," I said.

As we stood in the darkness, insect noises began – crickets chirped, and I heard a frog gulp in the dark water. An owl hooted. It was as if life were suddenly returning after the darkness of the demons.

I took Misaki back to the town. She sat on the cart with Cho, and we rode back through a clear night of stars and sudden warmth.

Her mother wept when she saw us. The other women of the town came from their houses one by one. Misaki was safe and they were happy.

"The demons are destroyed," I said. I stood and held Misaki by the hand with Cho by my side. It felt good to stand together – the three of us.

My horse nudged me, and I thought, 'very well then, the four of us together – my horse as well.'

The women made a feast for us, and we had rice wine. The women of the town were happy for Misaki and her mother, even though their daughters were all dead.

As the night went on we heard some noises coming from beyond the town, from the craggy hill, place of the demons. It sounded like girls laughing and shouting. Then we heard running and footsteps. It was not long before a group of young girls all ghostly in their white dresses were running towards us.

They were not ghosts. One after the other they ran to their mothers. "The spell really has been broken," I said, "and look, all of the girls are returned." It seemed that life too had really returned.

"Soon it will be the time of blossom," my brave Misaki said, above all the happy cries and tears and laughter. And she squeezed my hand then she smiled at me and then she patted Cho on his noble old head.

Our books are tested
for children and young people by
children and young people.

Thanks to everyone who consulted on
a manuscript for their time and effort in
helping us to make our books better
for our readers.

*If you liked **Samurai***

*then you'll like...*

# Ninja: First Mission

## Chris Bradford

He waits under the floor-boards. He's been hidden for over an hour, lying still as a stone. His name is Taka. This is his first mission as a ninja and he must not fail...

When the Grandmaster sends Taka on a special mission, this is his last chance to prove himself. But the mission is dangerous. To fail is to die, and Taka has failed before...

# Ninja: Death Touch

## Chris Bradford

An old man stands over Taka's shaking body. He is the Grandmaster of the ninja clan. And he has just given Taka the Death Touch...

Taka is now a black belt and is learning the lethal arts of the ninja. He will need these skills to protect his clan. Lord Oda has sworn to destroy all ninja. As Oda's samurai army marches on their village, Taka must fight once more, and this time his whole world is at stake...

www.barringtonstoke.co.uk

# More *myths and legends*...

## Thor and the Master of Magic
### KEVIN CROSSLEY-HOLLAND

The Giants are tricksters and cheats. The Giants would like nothing better than to attack...

Now Thor has come to take on the Giant King. Thor is strong and brave, and he is the God of Thunder. Are Thor and his hammer a match for the Master of Magic?

## Young Merlin
### TONY BRADMAN

Merlin has always known he was different from the other boys. But he has no idea just how different.

Inside Merlin, lies power.

Magic.

And that makes him a threat to the King...

## The Goblin of Tara
### OISÍN MCGANN

Every Halloween, the goblin comes to the King's great fort at Tara. Every Halloween, he burns it to the ground. Now Finn MacCool has come to take on the goblin. If Finn wins, he will become a legend. If he loses... how many will die?

Get ready for one horrific Halloween!

## Merlin and the Ring of Power
### TONY BRADMAN

Merlin knows his destiny makes him different. His power is growing every day.

But there are other threats to deal with.

The King.

And the Ring of Power Merlin must find to save the land...

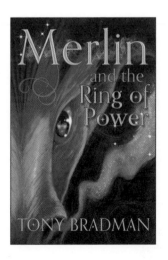

www.barringtonstoke.co.uk